STITCH HEAD

The Ghost of Grotteskew

CONTENTS

STiTCH HEAD

The Ghost of Grotteskew

by Guy Bass
Illustrated by Pete Williamson

tiger tales

THE BALLAD OF
MAWLEY CRACKBONE

His feet like thunder o'er the hill,
His fists for hammerin' pegs—
With a look of his eye you're surely to die,
He'll make you wet your legs.
Lo! He comes! Beware! Begone!
The monster, Mawley Crackbone.

His head's a rock for mushin' chops,
His breath like Brussels sprouts—
He'll put out your eyes for pigeon pies,
Or kill you with a clout.
Lo! He comes! Beware, begone!
The monster, Mawley Crackbone.

His coat's a bear, an' around his neck
A rattlin' ribbon o' bones.
He comes to town with a fart an' a frown
And whatever he sees, he owns.
Lo! He comes! Beware, begone!
The monster, Mawley Crackbone.

But sad the day of Mawley's end,
A curse on Grubbers Nubbin—
Not for the life he did misspend,
But for a costly bargain.
Lo! He comes! Beware! Begone!
The monster, Mawley Crackbone.

PROLOGUE

THE BARGAIN
(A timely end for Mawley Crackbone)

The moon was full over Grubbers Nubbin the night Mawley Crackbone met his timely end.

The townsfolk gathered around the body in a circle, not quite able to believe what had happened.

"Is ... is he really gone?"

"'Ard to know."

"He ain't movin'.... Poke him to be sure."

"*You* poke him."

"Not a chance! I ... I don't have a pokin' stick."

"Here—borrow mine."

"If you've got a stick, why ain't *you* pokin' him?"

"I ... I've been pokin' stuff all day! My pokin' arm's tired."

"*No one's poking anyone,*" hissed a voice. The townsfolk parted. A tall, wiry man in a long white coat slid into the center of the circle like a snake and stood over the body of Mawley Crackbone.

"We have an *arrangement,*" the man said. "Mr. Crackbone is no longer a problem for the people of Grubbers Nubbin ... thanks to my particularly potent poison. Now I am here to collect what is mine."

The townsfolk edged nervously away from the body. Then the mayor of Grubbers Nubbin straightened his tie and stepped forward.

"Of—of course, good sir. He's all yours," said the mayor. "But what do you intend to *do* with him?"

The man's lizard eyes flashed in the moonlight.

"That's my business," he replied. "A deal's a deal—no questions asked."

"Of course," said the mayor, retreating into the crowd. "And—thank you for your help ... *professor*."

"Don't thank me yet," said the man as he struggled to drag the body one-handed back up the hill. "You haven't seen the last of Mawley Crackbone. Ah-HAHAHAHAHA!"

CASTLE GROTTESKEW

Yesteryear
(Some time after Ye Olden Days)

STITCH HEAD
PLAYS DEAD
(Out of the shadows)

All the castle's a stage, and all the creations should sign up for auditions!

Signed, The Castle Grotteskew Creative Creations Collective Drama Society

"Ah-Haha-HAHA!"

As Stitch Head opened his eyes, Professor Erasmus's laugh rang through the dank, dimly lit corridors of Castle Grotteskew.

The castle had cast its sinister shadow over Grubbers Nubbin for slightly longer than anyone could remember. The castle was home to Mad Professor Erasmus, considered by most to be the maddest professor of all. He had spent a lifetime creating mad things, and each new creation was madder than the last. Though none of the creations had strayed as far as Grubbers Nubbin, the sound of the professor's laugh often echoed far beyond the walls of the castle to the town below, striking fear into the hearts of the townsfolk.

"Professor...," began Stitch Head, sitting up. "He's getting *close*."

Stitch Head wasn't scared, of course.

Not yet, anyway. He knew the professor's laugh better than anyone. He had heard it the moment he was brought to almost-life, when he was his master's first and only creation. Stitch Head had never been happier than the early days.... But that was hundreds of creations ago.

Not long now, he thought, *before his newest creation is complete....*

"Stitch Head, you're meant to be DEAD!"

Stitch Head looked up to see the Creature stride toward him. It was a massively monstrous creation, a colossal combination of mismatched muscles and the odd terrifying tentacle. The Creature was one of the professor's most recent experiments. It, like most of the professor's creations, had been quite menacingly monstrous until Stitch Head had cured it with one of his creation-calming concoctions.

"We've TALKED about this," continued the Creature. "I want you looking DEADER than COUNTRY DANCING...."

"Sorry, Creature," replied Stitch Head.

"IF you're going to be in the CASTLE GROTTESKEW CREATIVE CREATIONS COLLECTIVE DRAMA SOCIETY," continued the Creature, flamboyantly flicking its brand-new director's scarf over its shoulder, "you need to UNDERSTAND the rules of THEATER...."

Stitch Head sighed. He had never *wanted* to be in the Creative Creations Collective Drama Society. The thought of being in a society, particularly a dramatic one, disturbed him to no end. True, he had gotten tired of hiding away, deep in the inky bowels of his dungeon home, and he *was* eager to see what almost-life had to offer—but appearing in a play in front of all the other creations was more attention that he had ever wanted.

The Creature, however, had made up its mind. It was "time to step OUT of the SHADOWS! Time to MINGLE!"

Which was how Stitch Head found himself in one of the castle's largest, brightest halls, on a ramshackle set of tables and chairs, and surrounded by an odd assortment of the professor's creations—and, of course, the Creature.

"Now REMEMBER, Stitch Head, in this SCENE, you—I mean, your CHARACTER—is DEAD, so don't move an INCH, OKAY?" continued the Creature. "GREAT! From the TOP, everybody!"

"But—but I'm dead in *every* scene," sighed Stitch Head as the other creations busied themselves with props and positioning. "I *lie* here for the whole play. I feel so ... exposed."

"But you've got the BESTEST part! After ALL, what's a MURDER MYSTERY without a DEAD body?"

"Quite so!" noted a three-eyed brain spider. "I daresay you'll be reviewed favorably in the *Grotteskew Gazette* ... as long as you can stay absolutely still for three and a half hours."

"The reviews! Oh, Magnilda, don't remind me—I've got butterflies in my stomachs already," exclaimed a hulking hairball with coiled claws.

Stitch Head lay back down. He closed his eyes and thought of the professor, slowly bringing yet another creation to almost-life....

"Stitch Head...."

"What?" Stitch Head sat up again. The voice was loud and close—too close, as if it were right in his ear.

"STITCH Heeead...," sighed the Creature. "You're MOVING again! You look LESS dead than EVER!"

"But you said my—I mean, *someone* said my name ... didn't they?" he said, looking around. The other creations stared at him in puzzlement, and those of them that had heads shook them and shrugged.

"Let's go from the part where Stitch Head

is DEAD," announced the Creature, wafting its scarf dramatically. Stitch Head lay back down on the ground. He could have sworn he heard someone say—

"Stitch Head...."

"Who said that?" said Stitch Head, scrambling to his feet. The voice was even louder than before.

"Who said WHAT?" asked the Creature.

"That! I mean, my *name*," began Stitch Head. "I mean, I could have sworn I heard...."

"NOBODY said ANYTHING. Are you all RIGHT, Stitch Head?" asked the Creature gently. "Maybe you should take a BREAK— the PRESSURE of the PART could be GETTING to you."

"But—you really didn't hear anything?" asked Stitch Head. The Creature shook its head and patted Stitch Head on the shoulder.

"Don't worry—I'm not going to RECAST my BESTEST friend!" it said. "We can use an old CHAIR to stand in for you."

"Uh, okay.... I'll—I'll just go for a walk," mumbled Stitch Head. He shuffled past the other creations to the end of the theater and slunk through the door.

As he emerged into the corridor, Stitch Head heard the rumble of thunder. A storm was brewing in the distance. Out of a nearby window, he saw the dark clouds closing in, obscuring the bright morning sky.

"Stitch Head...."

The voice! It was closer than ever—so loud that it made his ears ring.

"Stitch
    Head....
        Give
            it
        back."

SOMETHING IN THE SHADOWS

(Spooked)

HERE LIES

MAWLEY CRACKBONE

WHAT YOU STARIN' AT?

S titch Head peered into the gloom of the corridor. At its far end, he could just make out a large, lumbering shape—a *something*, moving slowly toward him. Stitch Head would normally have thought nothing of it—the castle was filled with the professor's strange creations, after all. But something about this something made Stitch Head's borrowed blood run cold.

"Stitch Head…. Give it back."

Stitch Head froze, a strange shiver of fear running down his spine. Was it the professor's newest creation? He couldn't have completed it already ... and even if he had, how could it possibly know his name?

"Give it back," the something said again. It moved closer, and Stitch Head heard the rattle of dry bones.

"Who—who's there?" he replied. "Give what back?"

"Give it back.
Give it back.
Give it back!"

All at once, the something rushed toward Stitch Head with a mighty roar! Stitch Head screamed and turned on his heels, racing back into the theater as fast as his legs could carry him.

"You're BACK! GREAT!" cried the Creature as Stitch Head slammed the door behind him. "Ready to be DEAD again? Okay, let's get RID of the CHAIR—its acting is a bit WOODEN anyway...," it said, fanning its scarf.

"There's ... there's...," began a quaking Stitch Head, his heart pumping wildly. "There's something out there!"

"Is it the professor's newest CREATION on a MAD rampage?" asked the Creature, noticing fear in Stitch Head's eyes. "Shall I fetch your POTIONS?"

"I don't—I don't know," replied Stitch Head. He felt as if a huge, cold hand had his heart in a vicelike grip.

"Don't WORRY, Stitch Head, WE'LL protect you," boomed the Creature, striding toward the door. "WHATEVER that thing is, it didn't count on a ROOM full of ACTORS!"

"Creature, no, don't!" cried Stitch Head as the Creature swung open the door.

"AAAAAAH!" screamed the Creature. It turned back to face Stitch Head, a look of horror upon its face.

"What? What is it?" shrieked Stitch Head.

"I just REMEMBERED—we haven't REHEARSED the scene in the LIVING ROOM yet!" it cried. "Oh, and there's NOTHING there."

"What? But...." Stitch Head peered around the Creature.

The corridor was empty. Not a soul in sight, creation or otherwise.

"But—but I saw it," said Stitch Head quietly. "I heard it. It *spoke* to me."

"I wouldn't fret, deary—this castle is full of the most curious creations," said the brain spider. "I'm sure it was just one you haven't met before."

"It—it *can't* have been. It can't have been a creation," began Stitch Head, thunder rolling in the distance. "It looked ... *human.*"

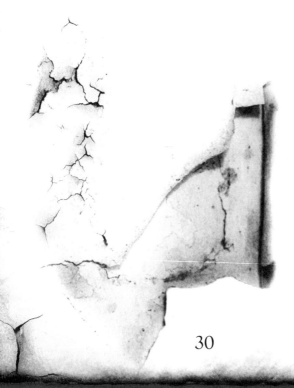

MADDER THAN EVER

(A visit to the laboratory)

MAD MUSING NO. 92

"A creation is only as good as
its ingredients."

From *The Occasionally Scientific
Writings of Professor Erasmus Erasmus*

Stitch Head and the Creature (who told its actors to "TAKE FIVE!" in the most flamboyant of tones) wasted no time in checking whether the professor had somehow completed his new creation sooner than expected. They made their way to the rafters above Professor Erasmus's laboratory. It was from here that Stitch Head had witnessed the "birth" of so many of the professor's creations.

"Can you SEE him?" whispered the Creature in a not-at-all whisper.

"Shhh...," replied Stitch Head, edging onto one of the rafters and peering down to the laboratory below. He could see the professor's bald head gleaming in the moonlight. "He'll hear us...."

"Ah-HAHAHA!" cried the professor. He was standing over a creating table three times bigger than any he'd had before. On it lay a huge, monstrous shape, covered in four or five sewn-together blankets. Stitch Head could see numerous tails spilling out from underneath.

"It isn't complete...," whispered Stitch Head. "And that *isn't* what I saw."

"AHAHA! Is it possible I've outdone myself yet again?" cried the professor. "Could it be that my creations just *keep* getting better? After my newest creation is brought to almost-life, I'll be madder than the maddest mad professor of all! Take *that*, Father! Ahaha-HAHAHA!"

"So if that human-looking *something* wasn't my master's creation, what was it?" muttered Stitch Head. "And what did it want back? I don't have anything to give...."

"What are you TALKING about? You have SO much to give!" replied the Creature. "You have a BEAUTIFUL SINGING voice,

you're GREAT at squeezing into NOOKS and CRANNIES, and you can MIX a monster medicine like NO one in the CASTLE...."

"That's not exactly what I—" began Stitch Head.

"ANYWAY, how can you be SURE you SAW what you SAY you're SURE you SAY you SAW?" continued the Creature. "I mean, there ARE no HUMANS in Grotteskew. The only things even SLIGHTLY human around here are YOU and the PROFESSOR...."

The Creature peered down at the professor, who was frantically trying to pry open a jar of eyeballs with his teeth.

"And I sometimes WONDER about him," the Creature added.

"But I heard it speak," said Stitch Head. He peered over the edge of the high rafters. "It said—"

"Stitch Head...."

Stitch Head's eyes grew wide. He turned to the Creature.

"Please tell me you heard that," he whispered.

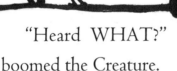

"Heard WHAT?" boomed the Creature.

"SSHhhhhH...." Stitch Head glanced across the rafters.

"Stitch Head...."

"It's here...." Stitch Head heard a bony rattle and felt fear gnaw at his flesh. He could feel the shape ... the *something*....

"Stitch Head...."

Behind him! Stitch Head clenched his fists and spun around to face his fear....

But there was nothing there. No shape, and certainly no human-looking something—just ceiling. Plain, boring old ceiling.

"But I could have sworn...," said Stitch Head. "What's wrong with me? Maybe you're right, Creature—maybe I'm imagining things. Maybe it's all in my head."

Stitch Head peered over the edge of the rafters.

A face peered back at him.

A *human* face.

"Give it back!"

"YAAAHH!" screamed Stitch Head. He stepped back, losing his footing on the rafter....

FACE-TO-FACE

(The workmanship is familiar)

MAD MUSING No. 654

"You only regret the monsters you don't create."

From *The Occasionally Scientific Writings of Professor Erasmus Erasmus*

"STITCH Head!" cried the Creature as Stitch Head plummeted toward the ground. Stitch Head barely had time to flail in horror before he landed with a THUMP!—right on top of the professor's almost-complete creation.

"Owww...," groaned Stitch Head, rolling helplessly down the creation's back until he fell face-first onto the cold, hard ground of the laboratory.

"Owwww...," muttered Stitch Head again, checking his strained stitches. He looked up at the rafters to see the Creature staring down in panic ... but no human-looking something.

"It was right there," said Stitch Head to himself. "Where did it—?"

"By my father's shiny bald patch! Who dares nosedive onto my most insane experiment?" hissed a voice. Stitch Head turned to see Professor Erasmus staring at him through piercing, lizard eyes.

"Master.... I—I'm sorry, Master," he muttered, scrambling to his feet. It was a rare day that the professor actually spoke to his first creation. It was even rarer for him to remember who Stitch Head was. Perhaps this would be one of those moments—perhaps the professor would recall their promise to be friends forever and greet Stitch Head with open arms....

"No visitors in the laboratory! No visitors in the castle!" snapped the professor, adding, "No visitors!" for good measure.

Stitch Head's heart sank.

"I—I'm not a visitor, Master," he said with a sigh. "It's me, Master. Stitch Head."

"What an absurd name," snapped the professor, giving Stitch Head a cursory glance. "Still, the workmanship is familiar...."

"I—I'm your first creation, Master. *You* called me Sti—" began Stitch Head, but the professor was once again distracted by his newest experiment.

"AHAHA! Am I not the most professoring of all mad professors? AHAHA! AHA! AHAHAHAHAHAAA!"

With that, Stitch Head may as well have disappeared into thin air. He shook his head. It seemed the professor would only ever care about his next creation, rather than his first. But Stitch Head knew theirs was a bond no one could break. He would remain in the castle as long as the professor did.

Or so he thought.

HAUNTED

(Debate at the dress rehearsal)

"No talent? No matter!"

Motto of the Castle Grotteskew
Creative Creations Collective
Drama Society

After a long day of being shouted at by the human-looking *something* (which seemed to appear out of nowhere and disappear into the shadows), Stitch Head's nerves were shredded. As he made his way to the theater for the dress rehearsal of the Creature's play, he felt as nervous as he was exhausted. He assumed his position on the floor and stared through a hole in the ceiling at the clouds that churned and rumbled above them.

The storm's getting closer, he thought. He felt a shiver down his spine ... and a moment later, a face appeared in front of him.

"AAAH!" Stitch Head shrieked before he realized that it was not the face of the strange something, but of his friend Arabella.

"Wow, Stitch Head, you scream worse than my grandma's cat when I threw it out the window."

Arabella was a girl from Grubbers Nubbin with a peculiar fascination for all things mad, monstrous, or downright terrifying. Unlike her fellow townsfolk, Arabella couldn't get enough of the castle and its creations—she made almost daily visits. It was as if she were impossible to scare.

"I'm sorry, Arabella," replied Stitch Head. "I'm a little jumpy...."

"What's going on? Has that prof of yours finished his latest mad creation or something?" asked Arabella, lying down next to Stitch Head in the middle of the stage.

"If only...," said Stitch Head.

One quick explanation later, Arabella seemed in no doubt as to the nature of the strange something.

"It's obvious," Arabella said, staring upward. "You're being *haunted.*"

"Haunted?" repeated Stitch Head. Thunder growled above them. "You mean, haunted by a ghost?"

"No, by a goldfish. Of *course* by a ghost," replied Arabella. "I mean, mysterious figure, appearing and disappearing, spouting nonsense and being a pain in the teeth? That's got *ghost* written all over it."

"POSITIONS, everyone!" boomed the Creature, its director's scarf flowing behind it as it stomped around the theater. "Don't forget, TOMORROW this room will be full to BURSTING with CREATIONS, all here to see you ACT your ARMS and LEGS off!"

"But ... ghosts?" said Stitch Head. "I mean, that's *impossible* ... isn't it? Ghosts aren't real."

"Impossible?" replied Arabella, raising an

eyebrow. "There's a three-eyed brain spider over there delivering a monologue. You're *surrounded* by impossible. This whole castle is impossible!" Arabella gave Stitch Head a friendly thump on the arm. "I'm telling you—you got yourself a ghost problem, plain and simple."

"What do I do?" whispered Stitch Head. "It won't leave me alone. It keeps telling me to 'give it back,' but I don't know what it wants...."

"You're in luck," said Arabella. "I'm an expert in ghost-kicking. My grandma's toilet was haunted by a poltergeist last year. It took me three days to send it packing. I've never met a spook that could stand up to my ghost-kicking boots."

"HERE we go! LIGHTS! MAKE-UP! ACTION!" boomed the Creature.

"Thanks, Arabella," said Stitch Head. "Right now, I'll try anything."

"Yes! It's ghost-kick o'clock!" said Arabella, clapping her hands together. "Pox, we're in business!"

"YaBBiT!" came a cry as Arabella's pet monkey-bat Pox (which also happened to be

Stitch Head's first and only creation) swooped down and landed on her shoulder.

"ARABELLAAAA, WHAT are you doing on SET? You and Pox aren't even IN this SCENE!" hollered the Creature. "In FACT, you're not in this PLATE at ALL!"

"*Play*, not plate, you dizzy dog-brain—and we've got bigger things to worry about," she huffed. "Okay, first things first, Stitch Head—what does this moldy ghoul look like?"

"I think—I think it's *human*," began Stitch Head. "But not like you. It—*he*—is huge ... and sort of see-through."

"Classic—ghosts love a bit of see-through," said Arabella. "What else?"

"Well, his face is craggy and worn, like an old wall...," continued Stitch Head. "And his hands are big and thick, as thick as stone turrets ... and he has a big, black fur coat and these rattling bones around his neck and—"

"Wait!" cried Arabella. "Did you say ... *bones?*"

"A chain of bones," confirmed Stitch Head. He saw something flash across Arabella's face that he had never seen before. It took him a moment to realize what it was—*fear.*

"What is it?" asked Stitch Head, another peel of thunder rumbling in the distance.

"We have to get you out of here," said Arabella. "*Now.*"

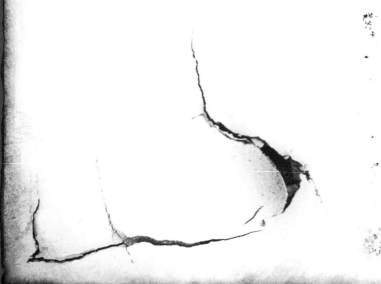

THE RETURN OF MAWLEY CRACKBONE

(Ghostly goings-on)

Best be caring, best be good,

Best be sure to do what you should.

Best be honest, best be kind,

Best your chores are done on time.

Best be decent and noble and true,

Or Mawley's ghost will come for you!

Within moments, Arabella was dragging Stitch Head through the castle, closely followed by the Creature.

"Stitch Head, WAIT! Your big SCENE is coming up!" cried the Creature. "The scene where you're DEAD ... still."

"Sorry, Creature, you're going to have to find a new corpse for your play!" said Arabella. "Stitch Head's got to go!"

"Go? Go where?" squeaked Stitch Head.

"Anywhere!" snapped Arabella. "Don't you get it? You're being haunted by Mawley Crackbone!"

"Who's CRAWLEY BACKBONE?" asked the Creature, racing after them.

"Mawley Crackbone! And it's a long story...," replied Arabella. "But if he's come to Grotteskew, one thing's for sure—we've got to get you as far away from here as we can!"

"What? I can't leave the professor!" cried Stitch Head, pulling away.

"And don't forget the PERFORMANCE is tomorrow!" boomed the Creature. "We NEED Stitch Head! The CHAIR just isn't COMMITTING to the PART...."

"Forget the play! And forget that old lizard! We've got bigger things to worry about!" snapped Arabella as thunder clapped above them.

"I can't!" said Stitch Head. "Anyway, I thought you said you were an expert in ghost-kicking. You said you've never met a ghost you couldn't—"

"Not this ghost!" shouted Arabella. "Not the ghost of *Mawley Crackbone.*"

Stitch Head couldn't believe what he was hearing. He'd watched Arabella fearlessly face off against a ship full of pirates ... seen her pick a fight with a ravenous octo-monster ... she'd even eaten a whole bowl of the Creature's cockroach, toenail, and belly-fluff quiche.... Arabella wasn't afraid of anything.

"He can't be *that* bad," said Stitch Head. "I think if the human-looking something ... if *Mawley Crackbone* was going to do anything, he'd have done it by—"

"Stitch Head...."

The sound was deafening! Stitch Head felt as if his head were going to burst its stitches. He covered his ears and felt something grasp him by the scruff of the neck. Suddenly, he was dragged backward, faster than he had ever moved, as if he were tied to a galloping horse. He screamed and braced himself to hit a wall or door or statue, but he just kept moving—*through* the wall. Faster and faster, through wall after wall and down through floor after floor, until he thought he'd never stop. Stitch Head closed his eyes....

Then, suddenly, he stopped moving. His head was spinning, and a now-familiar sense of dread filled his heart. He nervously opened an eye....

"Boo."

The human-looking something was staring him in the face! Stitch Head gave a horrified "YAAH!" and scampered back against a wall. He'd been taken to the castle's dungeon. He was home.

"Grutty puggler ... what are you, deaf? Mawley near lost his mind with all that hauntin' and hollerin'. Didn't you hear Mawley callin' to you?"

Stitch Head watched the "ghost" draw himself up to his full height. He was a slightly see-through mountain of a man, bigger than any human Stitch Head had seen, almost as tall as the Creature and impossibly broad and burly. His chiseled face was scored and pocked like the walls of the castle and he wore a thick bearskin coat, and a chain of bones hung around his sinewy neck.

"Mawley Crackbone...," whispered Stitch Head.

"That's right, puggler! And much obliged to you for sayin' it," growled Mawley. "Turns out you callin' Mawley's name aloud was all it took to give ol' Mawley a proper footing in the real world. No more fadin' in an' out like a poxy poltergeist! Ain't no ignorin' me now, is there, puggler?"

"I—I wasn't ignoring you," whimpered Stitch Head. "I didn't know what you wanted. I didn't know you wanted me to say your name...."

"Neither did Mawley!" boomed Mawley, rolling his tree-trunk neck. "How was Mawley to know? There ain't no manual for this ghost business."

"Y-you're really a ghost?" Stitch Head asked.

"Nah, Mawley's a goldfish. Course Mawley's a ghost!" growled Mawley. He leaned down toward Stitch Head and rattled the chain of bones around his neck. "Dead as the dry bones of my enemies. But thanks to you, Mawley's twice the ghost he used to be!"

Mawley picked up Stitch Head by the collar and swung him into the air—and through a nearby wall. Stitch Head squealed with horror as his head passed through the wall and a crate of Peculiarly Pacifying Potion before Mawley dropped him roughly back on his feet.

"Nifty, ain't it? Mawley can make you as ghostly as he is!" laughed Mawley. He reached for the crate of potion, but his huge hand passed straight through it. "But looks like that's still all Mawley can touch. Must be our *connection*."

"C-connection?" asked Stitch Head. "What connection?"

Mawley's fractured face contorted into an ugly grin.

"Mawley's body might've died a death,

but Mawley's *spirit* is still alive and kickin'. Somethin' called Mawley back to the world of the livin'. Took Mawley a dog's age to get 'ere, but Mawley gets what he wants, dead or alive."

"Called you? Who called you?"

"You're a dim little puggler, ain'tcha? *You* called Mawley!" laughed Mawley. He grabbed Stitch Head by the scruff of his neck, lifting him into the air, and pressed his ear to Stitch Head's chest. "Mawley heard you all the way from the Other Side. Thump. Thump. Thump."

"I d-don't understand," stuttered Stitch Head nervously.

"You've got something that belongs to Mawley," Mawley growled. He dropped Stitch Head onto the floor and then prodded him in the chest with a giant finger. "You got Mawley's *heart* ... and Mawley wants it back."

HEART OF THE MATTER

(The tale of Mawley Crackbone)

MAD MUSING No. 11

"A wicked heart is hard to find."

From *The Occasionally Scientific Writings of Professor Erasmus Erasmus*

"Your ... heart? How can I have your heart?" said Stitch Head, gripping his chest.

"Ask yourself, puggler," chuckled Mawley Crackbone. "Where do you think all your bits and pieces came from? Fell from the sky? You was *made*. Put together from leftovers an' spares an' borrowed bits. Your heart is Mawley's heart. Stolen by your master to make you."

"My master? How—how did the professor get your heart?"

"Mawley was hoodwinked!" growled Mawley. "Tricked into drinkin' *poison* by the ungrateful pugglers of Grubbers Nubbin."

"Grubbers Nubbin?" began Stitch Head. "Why would—"

"Who's tellin' this tale, puggler? You?" barked Mawley. "Now open your ears and shut your mouth. See, the folks of Grubbers

Nubbin didn't care much for Mawley Crackbone, though Mawley can't think why. They done a deal to acquire a mighty poison, a poison strong enough to finish off even Mawley. And they got it from a certain *Professor Erasmus*."

"Erasmus? But—" blurted Stitch Head, his eyes wide.

"He made the poison, and in exchange he got Mawley's unlivin' corpse for his experiments."

"The professor ... *took* your body?" said Stitch Head.

"That's how Mawley ended up in this castle," continued Mawley. "Your master got his hands on my heart and used it in the makin' of you ... and Mawley's glad he did! It gave Mawley a way back—a connection. So you see, you've got Mawley's heart. Time to give it *back*."

"But I—I can't give it back. It's … *in* me," said Stitch Head, feeling suddenly like an accidental thief. "I – I could get you another heart! The professor has dozens in his lab—and brains and arms and legs...."

"Mawley don't want another heart!" growled Mawley Crackbone. "Do you know how long Mawley's been floating around this castle? Fifty years! Fifty years of listenin' but never talkin', watchin' but never joinin' in.... It's enough to drive a ghost out of his mind!"

"I'm sorry! I don't know what to do! I had no idea...," replied Stitch Head, wondering if it could really be true. Did his master give him Mawley Crackbone's heart?

"What to do, what to do," growled Mawley, scratching his rock-like chin with thick fingers. Suddenly, his eyes flashed with an idea. It was such a pleasing idea that a wide, toothy grin spread across his face. "Looks like you and Mawley will just have to *share*."

"Share? I don't understand...," said Stitch Head.

"Why not? That heart joins us together. You and Mawley are like *family*," replied Mawley. "You ever had a family?"

"Well, I—" Stitch Head began.

KLUNG! KLUNG!

"Hey! You in there?" came a cry.

"Stitch Head, are you IN there?"

"I just *said* that!"

"I THOUGHT you were talking to ME...."

"YaBBiT!"

"Arabella! The Creature! My *friends*...," said Stitch Head.

"Friends, eh? We'll see," said Mawley with a shrug. "Well, what you waitin' for? Let the little pugglers in."

Stitch Head hesitated.

"Uh ... it's just that Arabella...," he began. "She's *scared* of you."

"Now what kind of grutty puggler would be feared of ol' Mawley Crackbone?" roared Mawley, clenching his massive fists. "What did Mawley ever do to her?"

"I—I don't know," replied Stitch Head nervously. "It's just—"

"No, no, Mawley gets it," huffed Mawley with a shrug. "Your *girlfriend's* got a problem with me."

"She's *not* my girlfriend!" insisted Stitch Head. "It's just it might be easier if—"

"Don't fret, puggler—even with a proper footin' in the world, there ain't nobody but *you* can see or hear Mawley," said Mawley. "Your girlfriend won't even know Mawley's here."

"She's not my—never mind," sighed Stitch Head. He shook his head and hurried over to the dungeon door and pulled it open.

"Stitch Head, we FOUND you!" cried the Creature, rushing in. Pox swooped in behind him, followed by an anxious-looking Arabella.

"YaBBiT!" yapped an angry Pox and immediately tried to gnaw on Stitch Head's leg.

"What's the big idea, running off?" barked Arabella. "One minute I had hold of you, and the next you ain't nowhere to be seen!"

"She's a bossy one, ain't she?" Mawley noted. "Reminds Mawley of himself as a young man...."

Stitch Head breathed a small sigh of relief. At least Mawley was right—it appeared no one else could see or hear him.

"I'm sorry I—uh—ran away," said Stitch Head, glancing at Mawley.

"We can't afford to waste no more time!" cried Arabella. "Mawley's after you—we have to get out of here!"

"It's true! Arabella says POORLY SNACKBONE is going to EAT you or BURN you or BURY you or YELL at you RIGHT in your FACE!" cried the Creature.

"Haw! Mawley's reputation precedes him," guffawed Mawley. "You goin' to let 'em talk about your *family* that way, Stitch Head?"

Stitch Head only managed an awkward "I ... I...," before the Creature conveniently interrupted with a question that he, too, wanted answered.

"Arabella, WHY are YOU so AFRAID of SURELY BACKBONE?"

"*Everyone's* afraid of Mawley Crackbone! Everyone that's got sense in their head, at least," Arabella replied. Then she took a deep breath. "Fine, I'll tell you the story if it'll help get you out of here…. But listen good, 'cause I hate telling stories, and I ain't telling it twice."

"Oh, I LOVE stories!" boomed the Creature. "Is it a HAPPY story filled with SINGING and FLOWERS and KITTENS?"

"It ain't," replied Arabella. "It's the story of a wicked heart."

THE TRUTH ABOUT MAWLEY CRACKBONE

(Heart of the matter)

MAD MUSING No. 811

"Insanity is a state of mind."

From *The Occasionally Scientific Writings of Professor Erasmus Erasmus*

"Wicked ... heart?" whispered Stitch Head to himself. He gripped his chest as Arabella began to tell her tale.

"Mawley Crackbone came to Grubbers Nubbin a long time ago, way back in Ye Olden Days. He appeared out of nowhere ... tramped into town with a mind to make it his own. One day was all it took for him to take over Grubbers Nubbin and crush the townsfolk under his big, horrible thumb. After that, he ruled the town like a king. Hardly anyone had the stomach to stand up to him. Them that did ... they ended up six feet underground."

"WHAT? Mawley made them live UNDERGROUND?" cried the Creature. "It must have been so DARK! Curse you, SORELY CLAPFOAM!"

"I mean they ended up dead!" snapped Arabella.

"Oh," said the Creature. "That's MUCH worse."

Stitch Head glanced at Mawley, who was awkwardly scratching the back of his head.

"Is—is that true?" whispered Stitch Head.

"Nobody's perfect," replied Mawley with a shrug.

"True? Course it's true! Mawley Crackbone was a *monster*," continued Arabella. "And not the kind of monster that you want to be friends with. He was the baddest, worstest, most awfulest wrong 'un ever! He wore the bones of his enemies around his neck! Mawley Crackbone's the only thing in all the world that scares the folks of Grubbers Nubbin more than Castle Grotteskew. He's the only thing in the world that scares *me* ... and I ain't never been scared of nothing. He was wicked—pure, rotten wicked right down to his heart and soul."

"Wicked heart..." murmured Stitch Head, his tiny hand gripping his chest. What did it mean? Did Stitch Head's wicked heart make *him* wicked?

"So Mawley wasn't no saint," grumbled Mawley. "Ain't you never taken over a town and ruled it with an iron fist?"

"No!" replied Stitch Head.

"Yes!" cried Arabella. "Look, Stitch Head, I know you like to see the best in folks, but there ain't nothin' good about Mawley Crackbone. Even after the townsfolk finally did him in, they was still scared of him ... scared that he'd come back from the grave— come back for his *revenge*."

"Codswallop! Mawley just wants his heart!" growled Mawley.

"It's not my fault!" cried Stitch Head. "It was—"

"No one's SAYING it's your FAULT," said the Creature. "But MAYBE Arabella is RIGHT—maybe we should RUN for the HILLS.... I mean, AFTER the first night...."

"Forget the silly play! We have to go!" snapped Arabella.

"What's the point?" replied Stitch Head,

his head spinning. "How can I run from something that's part of—"

"Careful what you say, puggler!" interrupted Mawley. "Do you *really* want 'em knowing the truth? You want *everyone* knowin' that you got Mawley's wicked heart beatin' in your chest? Don't you think they'd wonder, deep down, whether you was just as wicked as Mawley?"

"They'd understand...," whispered Stitch Head hopefully.

"Understand what?" asked Arabella.

"Your girlfriend's right, too—Mawley's done *bad* things," said Mawley. "Terrible, unforgivable things. Your so-called friends ain't goin' to want to know you once they know what you're *really made of*. You think anyone'll care how or why you ended up as part Mawley Crackbone? All they'll see is a wicked heart."

Stitch Head felt suddenly trapped. Mawley was right—if Arabella was this scared of Mawley's ghost, how would she react when she found out *he* was part-Mawley?

"GRuKK! SWaaRTiki!" yapped Pox.

"Pox is right, Stitch Head—we need to go *now*," insisted Arabella.

"Don't listen to 'em. You stick with ol' Mawley!" snarled Mawley. "We're *family* now. Families help each other! Stick with me, and I'll let you into a secret—a secret to set you free."

"I don't know.... I don't know what to do!" cried Stitch Head in desperation.

"Well, I do!" said Arabella. "Come on!"

"You can't run from who you is, Stitch Head," said Mawley. "Stick with Mawley, and he'll set you free!"

"HILLS!" boomed the Creature.

"Please, all of you, just stop...," said Stitch Head, gripping his chest tighter than ever. "Please, just leave me alone...."

"We ain't got time for this guff! Creature, grab him!" snapped Arabella.

"I said, leave me alone!" cried Stitch Head again. He pushed past Arabella and the Creature, ran out of the dungeon ... and kept on running.

GATHERING CLOUDS

(Confronting the professor)

"You can't make an omelet
without breakin' legs."

Mawley Crackbone

S titch Head didn't know where he was going. He just wanted to get away—from Arabella, from the Creature ... from everyone. He felt like the farther away he got, the less likely they were to discover the truth about his wicked heart. For the first time he found himself feeling something he never imagined he could—*anger* at Professor Erasmus.

He made his way to the castle parapet and watched the night fall over Grubbers Nubbin. He stared at the ever-gathering, ever-darkening clouds. It was as if they wouldn't move on, as if no wind would shift them. It was as if they were *waiting* for something.

"Enjoying the view, puggler?" said Mawley Crackbone, appearing out of the floor.

"*Please*, I said I just want to be left alone," murmured Stitch Head, instinctively holding his chest.

"Not an option," replied Mawley. "You still got Mawley's heart. That makes Mawley part of you."

"Is—is it true what Arabella said?" asked Stitch Head. "Did you really come back for revenge?"

Mawley laughed—a rolling, rumbling roar of a laugh that echoed in the thunder above them.

"Mawley couldn't get revenge even if he wanted to! Mawley can't even touch nothin', remember? Nothin' but you. Anyway, Mawley can't help bein' what Mawley is! You know the score ... you been thinkin' it all this time! Truth is, a wicked heart *makes* you wicked."

"No!" cried Stitch Head, his stitches fit to burst with frustration. "I don't *want* to be wicked...."

"The way Mawley sees it, you are what you

is," said Mawley. "You can't help bein' what you are no more than a cloud can help bein' a cloud, or a castle can help bein' a castle ... 'cause that's the way Professor Erasmus made you. He took Mawley's wicked heart an' he put it in you. Now you're wicked, too. Mawley figures if anyone's to blame for that, it's the professor."

"The professor...," repeated Stitch Head, gritting his teeth. He felt his rage burning inside him.

"Poor little puggler," sighed Mawley. "If only givin' you my heart was the *worst* thing the professor done to you...."

"What do you mean?" asked Stitch Head.

Mawley grinned. "Wasn't you listenin' back in the dungeon? Mawley's got a secret," he replied. "A secret to set you free."

"What—what secret...?" asked Stitch Head as Mawley closed in.

"Mawley's goin' to show you. Mawley's goin' to set you free," said Mawley. He grabbed Stitch Head by the arm and pulled him through the floor. The last thing he heard before the world went black was the rumble of thunder ... and the professor's cackling laughter.

THE SECRET

(Something in the room)

MAD MUSING No. 406

"All creations are created equal, but some creations are more equal than others."

From *The Occasionally Scientific Writings of Professor Erasmus Erasmus*

Stitch Head was pulled down through floor after floor of the castle. He passed through the theater, where the creations were gathering for the Creature's play, and farther, until he saw his dungeon home ... then farther still, farther than he knew they could go.

"Where are we?" whispered Stitch Head when they finally stopped moving. "What is this place? Are we *beneath* the dungeons?"

The room was almost pitch-black, and the air was thin, cold, and stale. Old cobwebs hung limply from the ceiling, and a thick layer of dust covered every surface. Not even the scuttling of rats or the distant cackle of the professor's laughter could be heard.

"This room's been under your feet all these years," said Mawley. "But don't feel bad— this is a place only *ghosts* can find. Mawley spotted it when he was clawin' his way back."

84

Stitch Head's eyes began adjusting to the darkness. At one end of the room he could just make out a small wooden door, and in the middle sat a small wooden slab, mounted on bricks. By its side lay a dusty old electric generator.

"Is that ... a creating table?" he said. He moved toward it and ran his fingers over the generator. "It looks ancient. What's it doing here?"

"Turn it on," said Mawley with a smile. "Shed a bit of *light* on the subject."

Stitch Head felt around in the darkness for the life-lever. His tiny hand settled on it, and he pulled the switch.

TZZ-KRKLE-TZZzzzzz!

The machine began to shake with life, and blue sparks of electricity forked out from inside, illuminating different parts of the room.

85

Near the door, Stitch Head could see a pile of mad science books and a small desk and chair. And at the other end of the room....

"What *is* that?" whispered Stitch Head, peering into the gloom. There was something there. Something *moving*.

"H-Hello? Who's there?" he said.

"Mawley promised you a secret to set you free," said Mawley. "Well, here it is."

Stitch Head moved cautiously closer. The something was small, even smaller than Stitch Head, and seemed to be cowering in the corner, shivering. It had two tiny, colorless eyes and a single spindly arm made from thin pieces of rusting metal. It pulled its ragged clothes about it as Stitch Head edged closer.

"You're a *creation*," whispered Stitch Head with a gasp. "Who are you? What are you doing down here?"

The creation stared at Stitch Head for a moment, as if it were trying to remember how to speak. Then it opened its tiny toothless mouth and forced out a rasping sigh.

"My ... name is ... Ivo," it wheezed. "I am first creation of Mad Professor Erasmus. I wait for him to come back for me."

THE PROFESSOR'S FIRST CREATION

(Wake up)

MAD MUSING No. 113

"A cackle a day keeps
good reason at bay."

From *The Occasionally Scientific
Writings of Professor Erasmus Erasmus*

"Wh-what do you mean?" stuttered Stitch Head. "You can't be the professor's first creation—*I* am."

Ivo struggled shakily to his feet, stretching legs he had not moved in decades.

"I wait for Master...," coughed Ivo, dusting off his clothes with his metal arm. He stared up at Stitch Head, hope glinting in his tiny, pebble-like eyes. "I wait in very small, dark room. I wait and wait for him to come back for me. Where is Master? Where is Professor Erasmus?"

"Why did you say you were the first— who are you? What are you doing down here?" asked Stitch Head. None of it made sense. How could he not have known about a creation almost-living here all this time?

"Why...," replied Ivo sadly. "Why Master lock me away?"

"Please ... that's what I want you to tell me!" replied Stitch Head impatiently. He gripped his chest as his heart began to THUMP, THUMP, THUMP. "How long have you been in this room? Why would the professor come all the way down here to create when he has a laboratory in the castle?"

"Please, not shout—is *quiet* down here in small, dark room. I hear fungus growing between cracks in stones. I tell you, I am Ivo. I am first creation of Professor Eras—"

"You're lying—you have to be," said Stitch Head. "You *can't* be my master's first creation. Professor Erasmus made me first. He *told* me!"

"Perhaps the professor wanted to keep this creation a secret," said Mawley, peering down at the desk on the other side of the room. "Perhaps he didn't want anyone seeing his ... early work."

"Early work?" said Stitch Head. "What are you talking about?"

"What I talking about? What you talking about?" said Ivo, oblivious to Mawley's presence.

"Take a look at this," said Mawley Crackbone, pointing down at the desk. "I'd pick it up for you, but, y'know, I'm a ghost."

Stitch Head hurried over to the desk to find a single piece of paper, covered in a thick layer of dust. He blew off the dust and held it up.

"No...."

It was a drawing of Ivo. Or rather, a blueprint—a plan for how to make him and bring him to almost-life. At the top of the drawing were the words:

MY FIRST CREATION
By Professor Erasmus E. Erasmus

MY FIRST CREATION
By professor Erasmus E. Erasmus

HEAD

NOSTRILS

RAGS

ARM
(METAL)

"It can't be...," cried Stitch Head as he felt his whole world begin to unravel. "I'm ... not...? It *can't* be!"

"No shout," muttered Ivo.

"*This* is why I brought you here," said Mawley Crackbone. "You had to see it for yourself."

"Why didn't you just tell me?" cried Stitch Head. "Why?"

"Have no met you before.... What I no tell you?" asked Ivo.

"Would you have believed Mawley if he'd jus' told you?" asked Mawley. "You had to see it for *yourself*, Stitch Head. You've been hidin' out in this castle for years, keepin' a promise to a professor who ain't bothered one bit about you. An' it turns out you ain't even his first creation."

Stitch Head shook his tiny fists. "All this time.... All this time I've waited for him to remember ... to *care*," he said, choking back angry tears. "But why would he? I'm nothing to him! Nothing! He didn't even give me a proper name!"

"Are you here to let me out? Please, let me out," begged Ivo, tugging on Stitch Head's clothes with his rusty metal arm. But Stitch Head could not hear him. All he could hear was the THUMP, THUMP, THUMP of his wicked heart ... and the voice of Mawley Crackbone.

"Poor little puggler," Mawley began. "I think it's time we paid a visit to Professor Erasmus, don't you? I think it's time you gave him a piece of your mind."

CONFRONTING THE PROFESSOR

(The sum of Stitch Head's parts)

Lo! He's back! Beware the beyond!
The ghost of Mawley Crackbone!

Mawley Crackbone would have taken Stitch Head to the professor's laboratory right then and there, but Stitch Head insisted they set Ivo free. Mawley made Stitch Head ghostly enough to pass through the door, and he quickly unlocked it from the other side. He pushed open the door, which creaked with decades of neglect, and stood in the doorway.

"You're free," said Stitch Head. "Go ... almost-live your almost-life."

Ivo stared at the open door as he watched Stitch Head suddenly vanish through a wall, transported by a ghost he would never see or hear.

"What is free? Is confusing...," said Ivo. "Is free same as sitting in small, dark room?"

Within moments, the ghost of Mawley Crackbone had conveyed Stitch Head to the professor's laboratory. For a moment, Stitch Head watched his master from the shadows, lurking behind a sideboard full of skulls. The professor's new mad monster had tripled in size since he'd last seen it—drip-fed a sinister cocktail of sizing serum, augmentation unguent, and a dangerous dose of Bigger than Before. The beast no longer fit on the professor's operating table and had been laid out on the floor, covered in ten or more sewn-together blankets.

"AhAHAHAHAHAAA! My maddest moment! My greatest creation—no, *the* greatest creation in the history of mad professoring!" cried the professor. He raced around his laboratory.

"What you waitin' for?" asked Mawley. "Erasmus ruined your almost-life before it even got started! You goin' to let him get away with that?"

"By my father's scaly back! All my other creations are nothing compared to this one! Less than nothing! AHAHAHA!" the professor cried, hugging one of the lifeless monster's four great legs.

"That *does* it," said Stitch Head, his heart threatening to THUMP, THUMP, THUMP right out of his chest. He strode toward the professor, clambering up onto his master's creation until he stood atop its highest point.

"Master!" he cried at the top of his voice. "You ruined my almost-life!"

"No visitors!" shrieked the professor, not looking up.

"Master!" cried Stitch Head again. "You called me Stitch Head! I—I thought I was your first creation, but now I know the truth! I am nothing to you! Less than nothing! All I am now ... is wicked! You gave me the wicked heart of Mawley Crackbone!"

The professor froze. He turned and peered at Stitch Head.

"The heart of Mawley Crackbone...," he repeated, a flash of recognition glinting in his lizard eyes, as if divining some distant memory. "Yes ... yes! I remember...," said the professor. "I used it for my experiment! An arm, a leg, an ice-blue eye ... and the wicked heart of Mawley Crackbone."

"It's true ... it's all true...," said Stitch Head, tears welling up in his eyes.

"If only I hadn't *wasted* it all those years ago," continued the professor, "I could have used a wicked heart for my *new* creation. AhAhAHA!"

"Wasted ... I've wasted my entire almost-life...," Stitch Head said, tears rolling down his cheeks. He fell to his knees and felt his own, unavoidable wickedness threatening to consume him.

"Told you, didn't I? You ain't never been nothin' to him ... you ain't never goin' to be.

You're just one of a hundred forgotten creations," said Mawley. "But Mawley can make you somethin—*somebody*—unforgettable. All Mawley needs is that."

Mawley pointed a massive finger at Stitch Head's chest.

"My heart?" asked Stitch Head.

"Mawley needs a body. Mawley needs to be *solid*," continued Mawley. "With your help, Mawley could be Mawley again. All you need to do is let Mawley in, willingly an' of your own free will."

"Let you in? But ... what would happen to me?" asked Stitch Head nervously.

"You'd be Mawley! *We'd* be Mawley! Mawley's spirit will make you strong ... powerful!" Mawley laughed. "Mawley will make you a *legend*. All you got to do is say the word."

Stitch Head watched the professor connecting power cables to his new monster. His eyes grew wide with frustration and rage. He felt the THUMP, THUMP, THUMP of his heart. Why pretend to be anything *other* than wicked? He couldn't escape who he was ... and he had nothing left to lose.

"*Do it,*" he said.

THE RISE OF MAWLEY CRACKBONE

(Stitch Head's surrender)

Never walk the streets alone
For Mawley's out and crackin' bones.

"Finally!" bellowed Mawley Crackbone, and the sky above them opened. Rain poured and thunder cracked and lightning shot down from the night sky. The wait was over.

"Hold still—this might tickle," Mawley said, rolling his neck until it cracked. Then he floated into the air, shimmering with a strange, spectral energy. His clothes, his bone chains, his whole body seemed to melt away before

Stitch Head's eyes until he was nothing more than a ghostly glow—a swirl of green light and fire. The glow moved across the room and settled upon Stitch Head....

"AAAAA-AAA-AAH!"

Stitch Head screamed so loudly that even Professor Erasmus stopped in his tracks. He turned to see Stitch Head slump limply to the floor.

There was a long moment of the most ominous silence. Then, slowly, Stitch Head rose to his feet and dusted himself off. He rolled his neck until it cracked and stared at his tiny hands.

"Much better," he said with a grin.

"Would you please stop all this screaming? You're ruining my professorial concentration!" cried Professor Erasmus. Stitch Head slowly turned his head and stared so intently that his master instinctively looked away. Suddenly, Stitch Head launched himself across the laboratory, landing next to the professor in three bounding steps. He pinned him against his desk, sending a dozen potion bottles crashing to the floor. A moment later, Stitch Head had grabbed his master by the throat in an impossibly vice-like grip.

"Unhand me! I don't have time to be

pelted or creation-handled!" the professor choked. He struggled wildly, but Stitch Head held him effortlessly in his grasp.

"Shut it!" growled Stitch Head, squeezing Professor Erasmus tightly around the throat. "Now open your ears, or this fist goes so far down your throat, it'll know what you had for lunch. See that monster of yours—it needs to be on its feet and rampaging in the next ten minutes!"

"Madness!" gasped the professor. "It's too unstable! It's not ready!"

"Then *make* it ready," replied Stitch Head, tightening his grip on the professor's neck. "Or for the first time in a century, Castle Grotteskew is goin' to be *without a professor*."

"Madness...," wheezed the professor again. "Have ... mercy ... Stitch Head!"

"*Stitch Head?* You'll be lucky!" laughed Stitch Head. "The name ... is Mawley Crackbone."

THE PLAY

(A surprise entrance)

CREATURE!

A MONSTROUS
MUSICAL MURDER
MYSTERY MELODRAMA

ONE NIGHT ONLY!

O n the other side of the castle, the raging thunderstorm was serving as a fitting backdrop for the first performance of the Creative Creations Collective Drama Society's production of *CREATURE! A Monstrous Musical Murder Mystery Melodrama*. More than a hundred creations had gathered in the theater to witness the spectacle, which was being met with equal amounts of confusion and bewilderment by its audience. Fortunately, they were all much too polite to admit they had no idea what was going on.

"What a ... unique spectacle," said a two-tailed skele-terrier. "I think all the SHOUTING really adds to the appeal!"

"I never knew plays could *be* so loud," noted a floating head with a clockwork brain. "What an almost-life-affirming experience!"

"I *especially* like the dead body," added a

loosely assembled collection of internal organs. "It looks almost *human*...."

"They're LOVING it!" whispered the Creature (very loudly) from the wings. "I was made for the THEATER! The ROAR of the GREASEPAINT ... the SMELL of the CROWD! My show is a HOT!"

"A *hit*—your show's a *hit*," whispered Arabella from her position on the floor in the middle of the set. She was already regretting filling in for the absent Stitch Head. She'd been playing dead for almost an hour, rain dripping onto her face from cracks in the ceiling. "Why did I agree to this? We should be looking for Stitch Head! We should be running for the hills! We should—"

BOOM

The sound stopped Arabella mid-moan. At first, she thought it was the storm, but then she realized it was coming from inside the castle.

BOOM
BOOM

"Is that part of the play?" she muttered,

trying not to move.

BOOM
BOOM

"ARABELLA, who's making all that RACKET? It's drowning out all the DRAMATIC racket!" whispered the Creature from the wings. "I SAID the creations should UNWRAP their SWEETS before the SHOW started...."

"This ain't sweets—and it ain't thunder, neither," said Arabella. "It's *footsteps*."

Arabella sat bolt upright. The audience (and the other actors) screamed in unison.

"The Dead have come to almost-life!"

"Is it part of the play or ... the End of the World?"

"AAAAAAAAH!"

"ARABELLAAAA...," whispered the Creature. "You're NOT meant to come to ALMOST-LIFE for three more ACTS!"

"Everybody, run!" cried Arabella. "RUN!"

BOOM!

The wall of the theater exploded! Vast chunks of stone and timber flew onto the stage, smashing the set to pieces and sending the actors and audience members scattering in terror. Arabella leaped to her feet, dodging out of the way as debris crashed to the ground around her.

Then, from out of the dust and chaos, came a *monster*.

"GRAAAIII

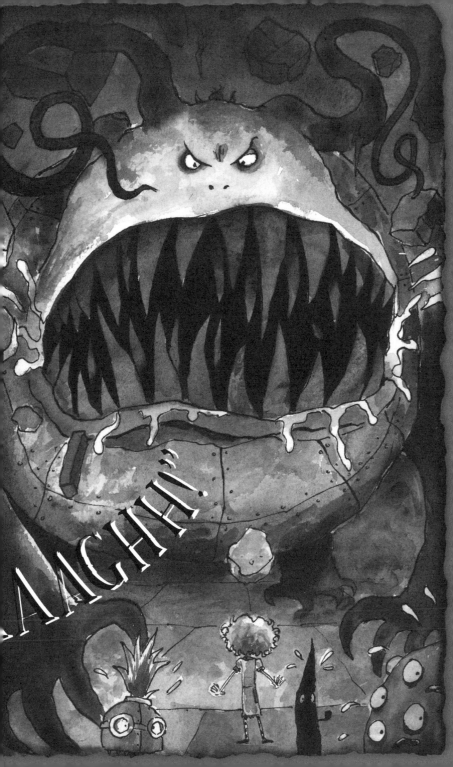

"The professor's CREATION," whimpered the Creature. "He FINISHED it EARLY!"

The beast stomped through the shattered wall into the theater on its four elephant legs. It was so huge that it filled the entire set. Half a dozen tails writhed around its gargantuan, metal-plated body, and atop its back the beast wore its own electrical generator, which sparked with electricity as it fed the creation almost-life-giving energy. It was by far the most monstrous creation ever to come out of Castle Grotteskew.

"AAAH! It's going to eat us almost-alive!"

"It's bigger than my bedroom!"

"Is this part of the play?"

"Run!"

"Slither!"

"Scuttle!"

"Roll!"

As the creations fled, the Creature watched in horror as the monster crushed the last of the set under its huge, clawed foot.

"Hey! What's the big idea, ruining a culturally enriching experience?" Arabella yelled. She shook her fist at the beast, enjoying the chance to be recklessly brave again. "Come down here if you dare! I've got a mind to polish my kicking boots with your big, stupid face!"

"ARABELLA! Don't PROVOKE the giant MONSTER!" cried the Creature, racing onto the stage. But Arabella took no notice. She rolled up her sleeves and checked that her bootlaces were tied.

"Come and get it, you tentacle-headed—"

Then she spotted it—something ... *someone* was riding on the monster's back. Arabella peered in horrified amazement.

MONSTER vs. EVERYONE

(Acting out of character)

"Revenge is a dish best
served with a side order
of punch-in-the-face."

Mawley Crackbone

"What's Stitch Head *doing* up there?" said Arabella as Stitch Head rode the mighty monster through the theater.

"YEeeHAaWW!" cried Stitch Head, pulling hard on two of the beast's tentacles as if he were guiding it by reins. "Now this is more like it! When Mawley Crackbone makes an entrance, he really makes an entrance!"

"Did he say...?" whimpered Arabella, unclenching her fists. Stitch Head looked down at the wreckage of the set to see Arabella, frozen to the spot.

"Well, look who it is—Stitch Head's girlfriend!" He wheeled the monster's head toward Arabella with a mighty wrench. "What are you waitin' for, monster? Gobble up that little puggler!"

"ARABELLA!" screamed the Creature, racing toward her as the monster opened its jaws. The shadow of the beast's great, fang-filled mouth fell upon Arabella as the Creature leaped.

"GOT you!" cried the Creature, grabbing Arabella just in time. They skidded underneath the monster, but the great beast's jaws snapped shut around the Creature's director's scarf.

"YURK!" exclaimed the Creature as the monster yanked it into the air. The Creature hugged Arabella to its chest as the monster thrashed its head from side to side.

Suddenly, Pox flew down from the ceiling and dove at the monster's head, sinking his teeth into the scaly flesh.

"GRAA-OW!"

The monster roared and flung the Creature and Arabella across the theater. They landed with a KRA-ASH! in the middle of the seating.

"You ... okay?" groaned the Creature, unfurling its arms. Arabella rubbed her head as Pox swooped down and landed on her shoulder.

"It's Stitch Head!" Arabella cried. "Something's happened to him. He thinks he's Mawley Crackbone!"

"And EVERYTHING was going SO well," moaned the Creature, inspecting its torn scarf.

"Useless monster! Mawley said *eat* her, not *play* with her!" snarled Stitch Head from atop the monster. "Finish 'em off—we've got work to do."

The monster took a deep breath. Its generator began to glow and smoke, and the beast suddenly seemed to be illuminated from within. It opened its mouth, and bright blue electricity began to spark around its fangs....

"GRRAHHAAAAHH!"

With a mighty roar, the monster launched a lightning bolt from its mouth. The lightning streaked out into the theater, and a dozen seats exploded in a fireball.

"Now that's what Mawley's talkin' about!" roared Stitch Head. "Burn it! Burn it all!"

"Wish I could do THAT," whispered the Creature, peeking out from behind a smoldering chair as the monster spewed lightning bolt after lightning bolt. Within moments, the whole theater was ablaze.

Arabella and the Creature raced to the relative safety of a nearby corridor and watched in dismay as Stitch Head steered the beast farther into the castle, burning everything in its path.

"I THINK you may be RIGHT, Arabella," noted the Creature. "Stitch Head is acting a little OUT of CHARACTER."

"It's the ghost of Mawley Crackbone! It *has* to be," said Arabella. "Mawley's got to him somehow, turned him wicked! But how? How did he—"

"Please to help me?" said a small voice. Arabella and the Creature turned to see a tiny, one-armed creation hobbling toward them on spindly legs.

"My name Ivo. I am first creation of Professor Erasmus," he said. "Please to help me find my master?"

THE BURNING OF CASTLE GROTTESKEW

(Stitch Head's in there somewhere)

How to Get Revenge

by Mawley Crackbone

You will need:
1 unwitting pawn
1 giant monster
1 secret
1 secret within a secret
1 town (for burning)

"What did you just say?" said Arabella, peering at Ivo. "Did you say you was—"

"I am first creation of Mad Professor Erasmus. Pleased to meet you!" said Ivo chirpily as the flames began to lick around the entrance to the corridor. "Is this your castle?"

"No, it ain't my—Forget that!" barked Arabella. "What did you—"

"Before today, I never see anything except very small, dark room," continued Ivo. "I think to myself many times, am I to spend whole almost-life in very small, dark room? Am I never to see flower and bird and amusing-shaped vegetable? Then I am scared I never see these things. But today I am free! In last ten minutes I see walls and windows and sky and rain and whole castle and hundred creations screaming, 'Oh, no, is fire, run run, help help, monster is coming!' Is fun! Is big day for me!"

"WAIT a minute.... YOU'RE the FIRST creation of Professor ERASMUS? No WAY! So is Stitch Head!" boomed the Creature. "WHAT are the odds of THAT happen— WAIT a minute...."

"Out with it, half-pint!" shouted Arabella. "How can you be the professor's first creation?"

"Is true! Look!" Ivo replied. He held out his single metal arm in which he held a folded piece of paper. Arabella took it and unfolded it.

"'My first creation ... by Professor Erasmus,'" she said, reading aloud. Her jaw dropped open as she stared into Ivo's tiny, colorless eyes. "Oh, *no*...."

Ivo's explanation was helpfully thorough— if a little rambling, considering the encroaching flames. Before long, Arabella and the Creature were beginning to understand the magnitude of the problem.

"So LET me get this STRAIGHT: GOREY SLACKBONE is a real, live, DEAD GHOST, who's ACTUALLY Stitch Head?" asked the Creature, scratching his head with all three hands.

"CHuRRuP!" snapped an exasperated Pox.

"Mawley! This is all his fault!" growled Arabella. "Mawley used Ivo to get to Stitch Head. Now Stitch Head knows he ain't the professor's first creation, that he ain't nothing special. Mawley made Stitch Head feel like there weren't nothing to almost-live for, and now he's got a hold over him somehow."

"But WHY choose Stitch Head? And HOW do we get him BACK?" asked a panicking Creature.

"I don't know, but we'd better think of something fast," said Arabella as flames began to lick down the corridor. "'Cause Mawley Crackbone ain't going to rest until he's destroyed *everything*."

Arabella, the Creature, Ivo, and Pox followed a trail of fiery destruction through the castle.

Wherever they looked, the castle was burning.

"I'VE got a QUESTION. HOW do we stop a GIANT, rampaging MONSTER?" asked the Creature as they pushed through hordes of terrified creations running in the other direction. "I'm WAY outside my COMFORT zone...."

"So many creations...," said Ivo, hobbling to catch up.

"A whole CASTLE full! THOUSANDS," confirmed the Creature. "Maybe even HUNDREDS!"

"And they're all going to be homeless or cooked unless we—*wait*," cried Arabella. "There he is! Get down!"

They rounded a corner into one of the castle's courtyards and ducked behind a statue of the professor. At the other end of the courtyard, Stitch Head sat atop his monstrous steed as it spewed bolts of lightning in every direction.

"Nothin' like a bit of mindless violence to clear out the cobwebs!" roared Stitch Head. "Burn it! Burn it all!"

"ChuRRuP!" yapped Pox.

"OH, Stitch Head, WHAT are you DOING?" whispered the Creature. "I blame MYSELF.... If ONLY I'd given him a PART with LINES."

"That's it, run!" Stitch Head roared, steering the monster toward a fleeing creation. "There ain't no hidin' from Mawley—hey!— what's goin' on?"

Suddenly, Stitch Head yanked on the monster's tentacles, pulling its head away from the creation. A lightning bolt spewed from the monster's mouth, decimating the Great Door to the castle—the door to the outside world.

"What's he doing?" whispered Arabella.

"Tryin' to claw your way back, eh, Stitch Head?" said Stitch Head, thumping his head with his fist. "Grutty puggler! This is Mawley's body now! You gave it up!"

Arabella, the Creature, and Ivo watched in bewilderment as Stitch Head started punching himself in the head.

THoMP! THoMP!
THoMP!

"It's Stitch Head!" whispered Arabella.

"I KNOW it's Stitch Head," the Creature replied.

"No, I mean, he's fighting back! He's still *in there somewhere!*" said Arabella.

They watched Stitch Head wallop himself in the head a few more times (THoMP! THoMP! THoMP!) before his eyes gleamed with wickedness once more.

"Yeah, that's right! Get back down into the darkest corners of Mawley's mind, where you belong!" said Stitch Head, grabbing ever more tightly on the monster's tentacle reins. He led the beast through the shattered remains of the Great Door, framed in fire, and out—out into the world beyond the castle.

"Enough of this! Mawley's got bigger fools to fry!" Stitch Head stared beyond Grotteskew, through the rain and wind and lightning, and spied the dim lamplights of Grubbers Nubbin. "Now *that's* more like it! Time for some *proper* revenge."

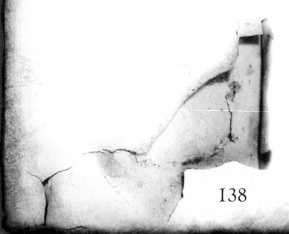

SAVING GRUBBERS NUBBIN

(Divide and rescue)

MAD MUSING No. 131

"The bigger the monster,
the madder the professor."

From *The Occasionally Scientific
Writings of Professor Erasmus Erasmus*

Arabella, the Creature, and Ivo watched with equal amounts of relief and horror as Stitch Head led the monster out into the storm—and toward Grubbers Nubbin.

"Every day is like this?" said Ivo. "Is exciting!"

"YaBBiT!" snapped Pox, trying to bite Ivo's metal arm.

"Okay, here's the plan," began Arabella. "Creature! Pox! Get everyone out of here, now! And then see what you can do about the whole castle-burning-down thing."

"GREAT! I LOVE an IMPOSSIBLE challenge," said the Creature.

"SWaaaRTiKi!" huffed Pox.

"Well, don't just stand there—get rescuing!" commanded Arabella as she hurried out the Great Door. "Half-pint, you're with me!"

"Is exciting!" squeaked Ivo, hobbling

after her. "We find Master?"

"Leave that to the others!" she replied. "Right now, we have to stop Stitch Head— I mean Mawley Crackbone—from burning down my town. We have to make Stitch Head remember who he is."

The commotion of a castle ablaze was more than enough to awaken the townsfolk of Grubbers Nubbin from their slumber. They were already panicking by the time they saw the monster stomping down the hill toward them. The beast seemed like an extension of the storm itself—lightning forked from its mouth and from the sky above, striking nearby trees or plowing into the ground. Combined with the sight of a burning Castle Grotteskew, it was as if the End of the World had come.

"AAAH!
A giant beast is
coming to eat us in our beds!"

"You're not even in bed."

"Well, not now—I got *out* of
bed to see the giant beast!"

"Your bedroom faces up the hill. Why
didn't you just look out your window?"

"Because it's—it's a giant beast!"

142

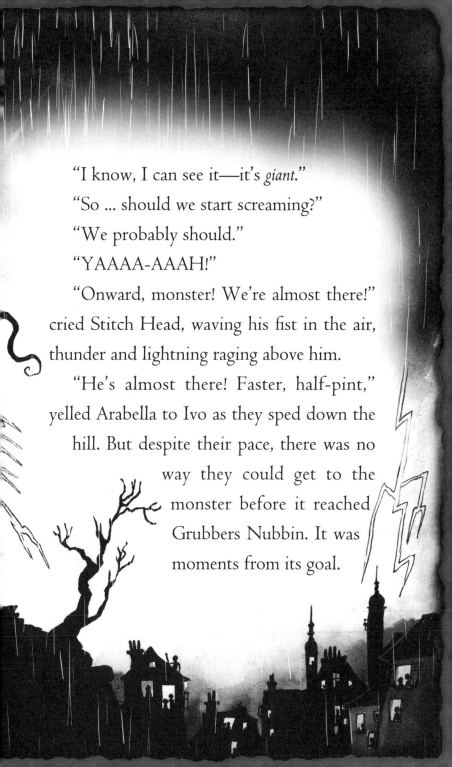

"I know, I can see it—it's *giant*."

"So ... should we start screaming?"

"We probably should."

"YAAAA-AAAH!"

"Onward, monster! We're almost there!" cried Stitch Head, waving his fist in the air, thunder and lightning raging above him.

"He's almost there! Faster, half-pint," yelled Arabella to Ivo as they sped down the hill. But despite their pace, there was no way they could get to the monster before it reached Grubbers Nubbin. It was moments from its goal.

"Mawley's waited a long time for sweet revenge on Grubbers Nubbin," roared Stitch Head from atop his monster. "What did Mawley ever do to them, besides a bit of manglin' and murderin'? Well, Mawley's goin' to make you regret—Hey!"

Stitch Head found himself yanking at the monster's tentacles again, pulling it away from the town.

"Knock it off, puggler! This is my body now! Mine!" cried Stitch Head, whacking his head as the ghost of Mawley Crackbone struggled to keep control of his limbs. The great beast began veering from left to right, zigzagging down the hill, crashing into trees and sending bolts of electricity streaking into the air.

"Knock it off, I say!" growled Stitch Head.

"Something's happening!" shouted Arabella, racing to keep up. "Come on!"

Ivo stumbled awkwardly down the hill, his thin, feeble legs barely able to keep up.

"The monster's slowing down!" cried Arabella, speeding ahead. "This is our chance." Before long, they were on the beast's heel, trying not to be trampled under its great feet or swatted by one of its many tails.

"Here we go!" cried Arabella. "Ivo, pick a tail and start climbing!"

"Uhhh, climbing is problem...," said Ivo, a little embarrassed. "I am only with the one arm...."

"Do I have to do everything myself?" huffed Arabella. "*Fine*. Hang on!"

She grabbed Ivo by his metal arm and swung him over her shoulder. Then she raced alongside one of the monster's tails—and jumped onto it.

UPON THE MONSTER

(Arabella vs. Stitch Head)

"If in doubt, wreck 'n' ruin!"

Mawley Crackbone

Arabella dragged herself and her passenger up the monster's tail, and then hurried along the beast's back to the sparking generator in the center of its spine. It was all that lay between them and Stitch Head.

"Mawley...," whispered Arabella, suddenly finding herself huddling behind the generator. Her bravado had evaporated. "Come on, feather guts," she whispered to herself. "Mawley Crackbone ain't nothing but a crummy old ghoul. You've kicked tougher and worser. Now get up! Grubbers Nubbin *needs* you."

But she did not move.

"When I stuck in very small, dark room," began Ivo, "I think, why would I be created just to sit in small, dark room? Then I am scared I will never leave. I will never see the flowers and the birds and the amusing-shaped vegetable. I will never almost-live. I think, is okay to be scared."

"I ain't scared!" snapped Arabella as lightning lit up the sky.

"But now I am free!" continued Ivo happily. "Things work out nice in end, angry girl. In end, we save your friend and your town and then I see my master!"

"Oh, yeah?" said Arabella, peering out from behind the generator. "And how exactly is this going to 'work out nice'?"

"I don't know...," said Ivo with a shrug. "Maybe we get lucky and bolt of lightning hit monster's generator. I have spent almost-life with nothing but small electrical generator for company, so I know electricity. Generator is like *magnet* for lightning. Maybe lightning will hit and maybe monster will explode in million pieces and town is safe."

"That's a lot of maybes," replied Arabella.

Ahead, the lamplights of the town illuminated the panicking townsfolk. Grubbers Nubbin was no longer in the distance, but right in front of them. Lightning flashed again, and in the middle of the street Arabella saw her grandmother, drenched by the rain and frozen to the spot with fear.

"Grandma...," Arabella whispered.

"Time to die, pugglers! Revenge!" boomed Stitch Head from his vantage point at the base of the monster's neck.

"Grandma! No!" cried Arabella, leaping out from behind the generator. She raced along the monster's back and threw herself at Stitch Head, trying to wrestle him away from his grip on the beast's tentacle reins. "Leave Grubbers Nubbin alone, you stink-faced hog!"

"A stowaway!" Stitch Head growled.

He released one of the tentacles and grabbed Arabella by the scruff of the neck. He swung her through the air and pinned her effortlessly against the monster. "Well, well—if it ain't Stitch Head's girlfriend!"

"I ain't his—Shut up, Mawley!" she cried, struggling to break free from Stitch Head's now-superhuman grasp. "Let Stitch Head go, you swine-stinking man-mangler! That ain't your body to take!"

"Mawley didn't take nothin'! Stitch Head gave up to the ghost!" laughed Stitch Head. "Now that puggler's no more than a nag in my head."

"Fight him, Stitch Head!" shouted Arabella. "I know you're in there! Fight him!"

"It's too late, puggler! He ain't got the strength to beat Mawley in a battle of wills!" growled Stitch Head. "Now be gone!"

With that, Stitch Head tossed Arabella into the air like a rag doll. She bounced helplessly off the monster's shoulder and plummeted to the ground.

"Angry girl!" cried Ivo, rushing out from behind the generator.

"*Another* one? This ain't a bloomin' cab, y'know!" cried Stitch Head. He spied Ivo and immediately burst into laughter. "You! HAW! You gonna pick a fight with Mawley, too, puggler?"

"Is too late to go back to very small, dark room...?" whimpered Ivo as Stitch Head released the reins and rounded on Ivo. The tiny creation limped backward, but it was no good—in a single bound, Stitch Head was halfway across the monster's back. He grabbed Ivo by the arm and hoisted him into the air.

"Please don't kill me before I have seen the flowers and the birds and the amusing-shaped vegetable!" begged Ivo.

"Kill you? Mawley should *thank* you! You played your part just perfect," chuckled

Stitch Head. "But Mawley *is* going to kill you, obviously. What say you join that kick-happy girly under the feet of this great beast?"

"Not so fast, Mawley!" came a cry. Stitch Head turned around to see Arabella standing at the base of the monster's neck.

"Huh? How on Earth—"

Arabella grabbed the monster's tentacle reins.

"Ivo!" cried Arabella. "Hang on to something!"

LIGHTNING STRIKES

(Ivo's purpose)

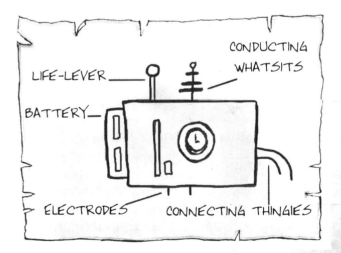

LIFE-LEVER

CONDUCTING WHATSITS

BATTERY

ELECTRODES

CONNECTING THINGIES

Arabella pulled hard on the monster's tentacles, making it rear onto its back legs. Stitch Head fell, bouncing and bumping down the beast's back and ricocheted off the generator. Ivo grabbed on to one of the generator's cables as Stitch Head tumbled past him.

"Grutty puggleaAAAAAH!" cried Stitch Head, plummeting to the ground.

"Angry girl! How did you—" Ivo began.

"Grabbed a tail on the way down! Now hold on, I'm going to try and steer this monster away from the town!" she replied, yanking on its tentacles again. The great beast roared in rage and shook its head.

"Knock it off, you bullying beast!" Arabella shouted as she was lifted into the air. "Rotten monster, turn back!"

But the monster did not stop. It crashed to the ground and fixed its glare upon the terrified townsfolk. Another lightning bolt struck a tree a few yards away, as if to remind the monster of its power. It opened its mouth, which began to glow and spark with electricity.

"Grandma! Everyone! Run!" cried Arabella.

Ivo, still clinging to the side of the monster's generator, felt the machine rumble and shake.

"Perhaps I am not meant to see the flowers and the birds and the amusing-shaped vegetable ... perhaps I am meant to do this." Ivo looked up as lightning forked down from the sky. He stared down at his spindly metal arm. "Perhaps *this* is why I am free from very small, dark room," he continued.

With that, Ivo clambered up onto the glowing generator as it reached full power and held aloft his metal arm. "I think is okay to be scared," he said.

As Arabella yanked on the monster's tentacles with all her might, she caught sight of Ivo on the generator, his arm stretched up into the air.

"What is he—" Arabella began. Then she remembered what Ivo had told her as they huddled behind the generator. "Ivo, no! Get down from there!"

But it was too late—a great bolt of lightning forked down from the sky, striking Ivo's metal arm. The bolt raced through his tiny body and into the generator. Then, in the fraction of a moment before the monster was about to release its blast....

BOOM!

The generator exploded! Arabella heard the monster scream, before the force of the explosion flung her off its back. She careened through the air and saw the ground race up to meet her. Arabella closed her eyes.

"GOT you!" came a cry. "AGAIN!"

Arabella opened her eyes ... and saw the beaming face of the Creature staring back at her.

"Sorry, I COULDN'T just leave you to TACKLE the monster ALONE," said the Creature. "Anyway, POX did a pretty good job of getting everyone OUT of the CASTLE, even if he did end up CHEWING a few of the creations...."

"Monster...," she groaned, sitting up in the Creature's great arms. Just ahead, still and silent in the driving rain, lay the monster. Upon its back, the blackened, smoking generator spluttered its last.

"What HAPPENED? One minute the MONSTER is going to DESTROY everything, and the next it's FAST asleep! I HOPE...," said the Creature. "Did you INTRODUCE it to your KICKING boots?"

"It was Ivo.... Ivo!" cried Arabella, struggling free of the Creature's grasp and racing toward the monster. "The little half-pint used his arm to bring down the lightning.... Where is he? Where—oh, *no*."

There, some distance from the monster, lay Ivo, charred, smoking, and still, his metal arm glowing from the heat of the lightning bolt. Arabella raced over to him and cradled him in her arms.

"Half-pint, wake up!" she cried. "You did it! You stopped the monster! Now wake up!"

"Is—is he going to be ALL RIGHT?"

whimpered the Creature.

"He—he ain't moving...," replied Arabella.

"Stop it," said a voice. "You'll have Mawley in tears."

There came a peel of thunder, and lightning lit up the sky. Arabella and the Creature turned around.

It was Stitch Head.

STITCH HEAD FIGHTS BACK

(The battle within)

"Takes more than bein' dead
to stop ol' Mawley."

Mawley Crackbone

"Well, well, ain't you a bunch of sneaky little beast-defeaters?" growled Stitch Head as he walked slowly through the rain toward Arabella and the Creature. "Never in all my years, alive or dead, have I met such gutsy pugglers. Not that your guts are going to save you...."

"Grotty ghoul!" shouted Arabella, cradling the limp body of Ivo in her arms. "Look what you did! Look what you've done!"

"He served his purpose," snarled Stitch Head. "He gave Mawley a way to turn Stitch Head against his master. A way for Mawley to guarantee revenge. It's *always* been about revenge."

"Stink-faced specter!" snapped Arabella, wiping the rain from her eyes. "Give us back our friend!"

"You ain't got no claim on him!" laughed

Stitch Head. "Ain't you worked it out? Stitch Head's Mawley, and Mawley's him! After the pugglers of Grubbers Nubbin did Mawley in, Mawley's wicked heart got put inside this stitched-together body. That's how Mawley found his way back to the world of the livin'!"

"No WAY! Stitch Head has the HEART of CRAWLEY FLAPSTONE?" gasped the Creature.

"Stitch Head...," whispered Arabella. "Why didn't you tell us?"

"Anyway, where was Mawley? Oh, yeah—revenge! And since it was you who stopped Mawley from burnin' down the town, Mawley's goin' to make an *example* of you."

Stitch Head strode toward Arabella, his fists clenched, a smile spreading across his face.

"Now, LOOK, Mr. QUACKBONE,"

began the Creature, stepping between Stitch Head and Arabella. "POSSESSING my BESTEST friend and BURNING down the CASTLE AND trying to DESTROY Grubbers Nubbin AND destroying my THEATRICAL endeavor AND ruining my director's SCARF is ONE thing, but Arabella is my FRIEND and it's not OKAY to—"

"Shut it!" growled Stitch Head. He grabbed the Creature by the tail, and then flung it through the air.

"YAAHH!" the Creature screamed, bumping and thumping along the ground.

"Don't you get it?! Mawley's stronger than he ever was! Mawley's unstoppable!" roared Stitch Head. He picked up Arabella by the throat as she clung on to Ivo's unmoving body.

"Stitch Head ... you're still in there, I know you are!" gasped Arabella as Stitch Head held her aloft. "You ain't nothing—you're our friend! Whoever you were then, right now you're ... still our ... friend...."

Arabella's world grew black as Stitch Head's impossibly strong fingers tightened around her neck. She felt herself drop Ivo to the ground.

"Stitch Head's gone," snarled Stitch Head. "No more than a thought in the back of Mawley's—Huh?"

Stitch Head shook his head, and with his free hand he suddenly punched himself in the face. "No! Not again! Get back in there!" he growled.

Arabella felt Stitch Head's grip relax. Lightning lit up the sky, and she saw a familiar, pained look in Stitch Head's eyes. "That's ... it ... fight...," she gasped.

"No! No no NO!" roared Stitch Head, thumping himself in the head again. "This is Mawley's body! Mawley's heart! Mawley's revenge!"

"STITCH HEAD!" came a booming cry. Stitch Head turned to see the Creature, struggling to its feet. "STOP! You're my BESTEST friend! BESTEST friends don't STRANGLE each other!"

"Shut up!" snarled Stitch Head. "This ain't none of your business! The deal's done! Ain't no one beatin' Mawley—Mawley's unstoppable! Mawley's—AAAAAAH!"

Suddenly, Stitch Head released Arabella, dropping her to the ground.

"Fight...," she panted.

"Wait ... wait!" cried Stitch Head. He fell to his knees and grabbed the sides of his head. "Let's—let's talk about this! Mawley's made you unstoppable! Unforgettable! Do you want to go back to bein' nothin'? You're not even the professor's first creation! Stick with Mawley! We—we can share!"

Stitch Head roared in pain again, pressing his palms against his head. For a moment, it seemed as if he might burst his stitches. Then, as the rain lashed against him, he began to glow with a strange green light.

"WHAT'S happening to Stitch Head? I mean, to CHORLEY FATCRONE?" asked the Creature.

"You rotten, ungrateful puggler!" he screamed. "I want my heart back! I want my life back! I want revenge! Wait, please, wait! Give me another chance! Please, waaAAAAAAAAAITT!"

Stitch Head craned backward and cast his eyes to the sky. Suddenly, the light began to pour out of him like liquid. The light began to pool above his head in a vivid green halo. Then, as Stitch Head stared upward, the light took shape....

"Mawley...," coughed Arabella. Sure enough, for all to see, the ghost of Mawley Crackbone had appeared. For a moment, he simply hovered in the air, trying to find a way back. Then, as he looked down at Stitch Head, he began to disappear.

"Grutty puggler! I had you right where I wanted you! I had you beaten!" growled Mawley. "How d'you do it? Grutty puggler, give me back my heart!"

"Mawley," said Stitch Head. "Leave me *alone*."

And with that, Mawley Crackbone vanished.

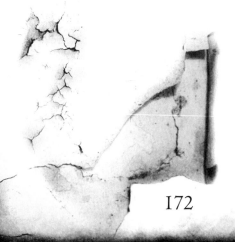

THE TWENTY-FIRST CHAPTER

RETURN TO THE CASTLE

(Back to Ghost Land, or wherever)

MAD MUSING No. 717

"There are no such things as ghosts. Monsters, werewolves, vampires, and zombies, yes. But ghosts? Madness!"

From *The Occasionally Scientific Writings of Professor Erasmus Erasmus*

No sooner had the ghost of Mawley Crackbone evaporated into thin air than Stitch Head slumped to the ground.

"Stitch Head!" cried Arabella as she and the Creature raced over to him.

"Wake up, Stitch Head. Stitch Head, wake up...," said Arabella softly.

Stitch Head opened his eyes and saw the faces of his friends looking down at him.

"STITCH HEAD?" whispered the Creature. "Uh, it IS you, ISN'T it?"

"I—I think so.... I *hope* so," replied Stitch Head, sitting up. "What happened?"

"We saw RORY SNACKBOWL!" boomed the Creature. "He was THERE, then he WASN'T. Do you THINK he's gone BACK to GHOST LAND? Or WHEREVER it is ghosts GO...."

"I'm ... not sure," replied Stitch Head,

rubbing his temples. "But he's gone."

"You beat him," said Arabella, not quite able to believe it. "You beat Mawley."

Stitch Head looked up and saw the great black clouds begin to part. The rain now fell in a patter of light drops upon the ground, and the sky brightened before his eyes—the storm was passing. For a moment he felt at peace ... but then he remembered.

"The castle!" he cried, turning around. At the top of the hill, Grotteskew lay in ruins. Dense plumes of black smoke poured out from inside, filling the sky.

"What have I done?" he said.

"We got EVERYONE out," said the Creature, eager to look on the bright side. "And the RAIN seems to have done a DECENT job of putting OUT the FIRE, at LEAST."

"I destroyed it...," whispered Stitch Head, a tear running down his cheek.

"Ain't no use worrying about that now," replied Arabella, looking around. The townsfolk were starting to move closer, their fear and suspicion bubbling into anger. "We should get you out of here before things turn ugly. The folks of Grubbers Nubbin ain't very happy about creations being in their town."

Stitch Head struggled to his feet and noticed something lying on the ground. It was a small, lifeless figure.

"Ivo...."

"He saved us," said Arabella with a sniff. "He used his arm to bring the lightning—he stopped the monster."

"It's my fault," said Stitch Head as the Creature scooped Ivo gently into all three of its arms. "I didn't mean for any of this to happen.... I've destroyed *everything!*"

"Stitch Head, we've got to go," said Arabella as the townsfolk closed in. She saw her grandmother in the crowd, struggling to get to her. "Don't worry, Grandma, I'll be back for dinner!" she added.

"Arabella Guff, where are you going with those mad things?" called Arabella's grandmother sternly.

"Your SURNAME is GUFF?" giggled the Creature.

"These kicking boots are still good for

another few bouts," snarled Arabella. "Now come on, let's get out of here."

Arabella dragged Stitch Head back up the hill as fast as she could. The Creature followed behind, with Ivo held tightly to its chest.

"I destroyed everything...," whispered Stitch Head. He looked up at what remained of the castle, smoldering in the brightening dawn light.

"It ain't your fault, Stitch Head. Mawley Crackbone did this. He made you think you wasn't the professor's—y'know...," Arabella said.

"His first creation—because I'm *not*...," said Stitch Head, glancing up at Ivo, nestled in one of the Creature's enormous hands. "I can't change that. I can't change what I've done ... but I have to try and put things *right*. I have a chance to save Ivo."

BACK TO ALMOST-LIFE

(Charge up the generators)

MAD MUSING NO. 59

"The end of a life is the beginning
of an experiment."

From *The Occasionally Scientific
Writings of Professor Erasmus Erasmus*

By the time Stitch Head, Arabella, and the Creature reached the castle, a hundred or more creations had gathered outside, evacuated from the castle by a relentless Pox, but desperate not to stray too far from their home. Pox continued swooping and dive-bombing the crowds, like a particularly bad-tempered sheepdog.

"The CASTLE doesn't look so BAD now that it's NOT a RAGING INFERNO," said the Creature, trying to stay positive.

"All these creations—where will they go? What have I done? Master, I'm so sorry...," began Stitch Head. "Master? Where is he? Where's the professor?"

"He didn't want to LEAVE his LABORATORY, so I DRAGGED him OUTSIDE just before I came after YOU...," answered the Creature. It pointed to a large sack, hanging from a tree not far from what remained of the castle entrance. It squirmed and grumbled in a strangely familiar fashion.

"I DON'T think he EVEN knows what HAPPENED," added the Creature, plucking the sack from the tree. "Although it's PROBABLY a bit STUFFY in there...."

"Bring him along.... But don't let him out—not yet. It's probably best if he doesn't see the castle from the outside," said Stitch Head guiltily. "Anyway, we have work to do."

+ +

As they made their way through the castle, Stitch Head realized the full extent of the damage. Almost every inch had been blackened and scarred by the flames. As impossible as it seemed, it now looked even gloomier. It would take months to restore—but Stitch Head couldn't worry about that now. He had a creation to save.

Fortunately, the professor's laboratory, deep in the center of the castle, was more or less intact. As he pushed open the door, Stitch Head was relieved to find that but for some charring and singeing, it looked very much as it did before the blaze. He took a deep breath.

"Can I do this?" he whispered to himself. Stitch Head had witnessed the "birth" of dozens of the professor's creations and had cured almost as many of their monstrousness with one potion or another. He knew almost as much about mad science as his master. But could he bring a creation *back* to almost-life? There was only one way to find out. Stitch Head clenched his fists.

"Charge up the generators!" he cried, rushing into the laboratory. "Arabella, get me two of those blue potion bottles and six of the red! Creature, lay Ivo down on that table over there."

The Creature dropped the professor-filled sack in the corner of the laboratory before carefully laying Ivo on a creating table in the center of the room. Stitch Head set about preparing for the experiment. He worked tirelessly for hours, drawing up plans, testing theories, assembling contraptions, and mixing potions.

By nightfall, every inch of the room was a mass of strange machines and potion bottles, bubbling over with miraculous concoctions. And in the center of the room, not far from where Ivo lay, was an electrical generator.

With everything in place, Stitch Head stood over the body of Ivo, exhausted and wide-eyed. The Creature, Arabella, and Pox (who had grown tired of hassling the castle's creations) watched from a safe distance.

"Stand by," he said, attaching the last of the potion pump cables.

"You can DO it, Stitch Head!" cried the Creature.

"*Please work,*" added Arabella.

"SWaRTiKi!" barked Pox.

Stitch Head wrapped a tiny hand around the generator's life-lever and held his breath.

"Live," he whispered ... and pulled the life-lever.

FTZZ-KRAcKLE-TzZZZAZ!

"More power! More!" shouted Stitch Head as Ivo's body was bombarded with electricity for the second time that day. He jammed the life-lever down as the generator shook uncontrollably.

"The Lively Revival Brew! I almost forgot!" cried Stitch Head. He grabbed a vial of glowing green potion and glugged it into the potion pump. Now Ivo, too, began to shake as the Lively Revival Brew flowed through his veins. The generator quickly began to spark and smoke. Stitch Head held the life-lever firmly and shouted, "Everyone, get down!"

"Stitch Head!" cried Arabella as the generator exploded.

KkLE-zZZZkAkoOOM!

"Stitch Head...?" said Arabella again. Then, as the smoke began to clear, Stitch Head struggled to his feet, the life-lever (minus its generator) still firmly gripped in his fist.

"Now THAT is MAD professoring," exclaimed an impressed Creature as Stitch Head limped back over to the creating table.

But did it work? thought Stitch Head, lifting the still-limp body of Ivo by the shoulders. "Ivo! Ivo, can you hear me? I brought you back! Ivo!"

But Ivo remained still.

"But I brought you back...," said Stitch Head. He sighed a long, defeated sigh and gently laid Ivo down on the creating table. He closed his eyes, and with the last of his hope dwindling away, he whispered, "Ivo, wake up. Wake up, Ivo."

There was silence. Then,

"Master...?"

"Stitch Head, look!" shouted Arabella as she and the Creature raced toward them. Stitch Head opened his eyes.

Ivo was sitting up.

He was *alive!*

Almost.

Again!

MASTER, MEET CREATION

(Letting the professor out of the bag)

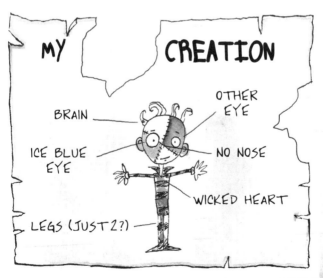

MY CREATION

BRAIN

OTHER EYE

ICE BLUE EYE

NO NOSE

WICKED HEART

LEGS (JUST 2?)

"M aster?" said Ivo again, rubbing his head with his spindly metal arm.

"Ivo, you're almost-alive!" cried Stitch Head as everyone gathered around.

"SWaRTiKi!" barked Pox, swooping down from the rafters and landing on Arabella's shoulder.

"What happened?" began Ivo as Stitch Head and Arabella helped him down from the creating table. "I remember doing heroic, selfless act, then nothing. Where is Master?"

"Your master! He's here, Ivo!" said Stitch Head. "Creature, I think it's time to let the professor out...."

"OKAY, but DON'T blame ME if he's a little GRUMPY—he's been in that SACK for SEVEN hours...," replied the Creature.

The Creature fetched the sack from the corner of the room and tipped it upside down.

The professor spilled out with a THUD-UMP!

"AAAAaaaHooo *Outrage!*" screamed the professor, gasping for air and flailing wildly. "What is the meaning of this? I'm in the middle of an incredibly important experiment! Or I was, until someone made me bring my creation to—"

"Professor...," began Stitch Head, walking slowly toward him. No sooner had the professor seen Stitch Head than he leaped to his feet, wailing madly. "You! AAH! AaaAAH! You made me awaken my creation before it was ready! You manhandled me at a critical point in the creating process! Stay away from me!"

"Master, I am sorry for what happened ... for what I did," said Stitch Head. "I know I can never make up for it, but I promise I'll try to put things right ... starting now."

"Leave me alone! Stay away! I must complete my creation!" raged the professor. Stitch Head felt strange. As much as he hated what he had become under Mawley Crackbone's thrall, at least the professor now knew who he was! But it wasn't *him* the professor needed to remember. Stitch Head took a long, deep, breath.

"Professor, please—*please* listen to me,"
pleaded Stitch Head. "There's someone
who's been waiting a long time to meet you
... again."

He gestured for Ivo to step forward.

"Ivo, here is Professor
Erasmus, your master,"
began Stitch Head.
"Professor, here is Ivo,
your ... first creation."

"That little thing?" huffed the professor. "It doesn't look familiar...."

Stitch Head furrowed his brow and glanced at Ivo with a sympathetic nod.

"He gets confused ... he doesn't mean to hurt your feelings," Stitch Head said, and then turned back to the professor. "Master ... Professor, Ivo *is* your first creation. You made him and you brought him to almost-life and that has to count for something. It doesn't matter how many creations you've made or how impressive they are—you can't just forget about them. You have a responsibility to *all* of your creations. And especially to him ... *especially* to your first creation."

Professor Erasmus turned to Ivo, who was peering at the professor intently through his tiny, colorless eyes.

"Hmph ... there is some naïve artistry

there—I suppose he *could* be my first creation...," he said with a shrug.

"Thank you, Professor," Stitch Head said, breathing a rather sad sigh of relief.

"Is impossible," said Ivo matter-of-factly. "That is not Master."

"Wh-what?" blurted Stitch Head.

"That," Ivo replied, "is *not* Professor Erasmus."

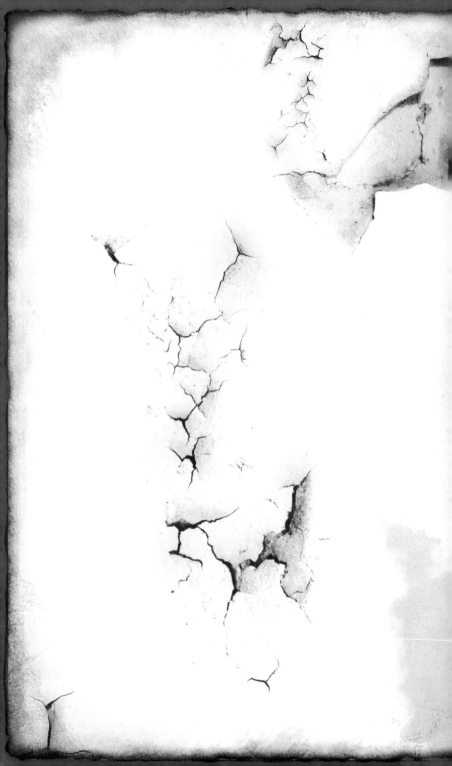

PROFESSORS PLURAL

(Mawley's secret plan)

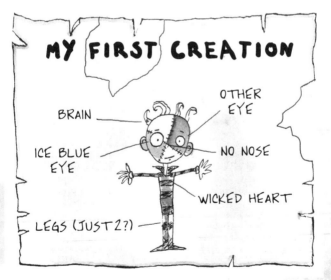

MY FIRST CREATION

BRAIN

OTHER EYE

ICE BLUE EYE

NO NOSE

WICKED HEART

LEGS (JUST 2?)

"Has been many years since I saw Master, but I remember like was yesterday," said Ivo, pointing at the professor with his one arm. "That is not Professor Erasmus."

"That lightning bolt must have messed up your marbles, half-pint," scoffed Arabella. "Everybody *knows* that's Erasmus!"

"But Professor Erasmus only has *one arm*," Ivo stated. "Like me."

"One arm?" repeated Stitch Head.

"And HERE I am with LIMBS to SPARE—AWKWARD," whispered the Creature, hiding his third arm under his coat.

"One arm ... one arm...," said the professor to himself as he stared into an empty bottle of Lively Revival Brew. His lizard eyes flashed with recognition once again. A thin, almost-smile spread across his face. "Do you know, my *father* had only one arm."

"Wait, what?" said Stitch Head.

"My father—Professor Erasmus," continued the professor, his mad mind all-too-briefly clear. "I remember ... *his* father didn't want him to be a mad professor, he wanted him to go into the family business—accounting! Ahaha! What madness! I remember Father telling me how he had to conduct his first experiment in *hiding*, deep underground...."

"Professor Erasmus ... the *first* Professor Erasmus!" said Stitch Head, the truth slowly dawning upon him.

"I watched my father as a child—AhaA!—here in the laboratory...," continued the professor in a nostalgic daydream. "He gave me all the things I would need for my *own* experiment ... an arm, a leg, an ice-blue eye, a wicked heart...."

"Of course! It's so obvious!" cried Arabella.

"I KNOW, SO obvious!" cried the Creature. "Wait, WHAT'S obvious?"

"Don't you get it? The prof's dad was a mad professor, too! He was the *first* Mad Professor Erasmus!" explained Arabella.

"WAIT, there are MAD professors PLURAL?" groaned the Creature. "My HEAD hurts...."

"Then the professor's drawing ... the room underground...," Stitch Head began.

"Exactly! Ivo wasn't this professor's first creation—he was the work of the professor's *dad!*" continued Arabella. "That was Mawley's secret plan all along—to make you believe Ivo was something he wasn't. Mawley *tricked* you, Stitch Head. He tricked you into giving up everything."

"So Ivo has been unknowing pawn in battle for heart and mind? Really is big day for me!"

exclaimed Ivo. "But wait, where is *my* master?"

"Hate to say it, half-pint, but your old prof has been six feet underground for years," said Arabella. "And I ain't talking about a very small, dark room—I mean he's dead and gone."

"DEADER than COUNTRY DANCING," added the Creature, putting his third hand on Ivo's shoulder. "But DON'T worry, you've got US now! We can ALL be BESTEST friends TOGETHER! Isn't that GREAT?"

"I suppose," replied Ivo, wiping a tear from his eye. "But can I ask, is almost-life in castle always filled with monsters and running and screaming and terror?"

"PRETTY much!" replied the Creature.

Stitch Head, meanwhile, watched the professor wander around the laboratory, lost in memory, muttering about his first creation, and, of course, his next.

"Master," he whispered to himself, and smiled. With that, Stitch Head and his friends made their way out of the laboratory and through what remained of the castle.

"You okay, Stitch Head?" asked the Creature. "You're QUIETER than USUAL, and that's SAYING something."

"I don't know, Creature," Stitch Head replied, lifting a hand to his chest. "Yesterday, I felt like I didn't know who I was. Now I'm not sure it *matters* who I am."

"What matters is what you *do*, Stitch Head," said Arabella as the Creature and Ivo gathered around them. "It don't matter how you're made. You can be a man or a monster ... you can have tentacles or tails, wings or fangs, one arm or a wicked heart ... none of that matters. You decide what you do, and that *makes* you who you are."

"YaBBiT!" agreed Pox. Stitch Head looked around at the blackened walls.

"In that case, I'd better get to work—I have a castle to rebuild," he said. "All these years

I've worried about the professor, but from now on, I need to think about his creations. This is their home. They have nowhere else to go. No matter how long it takes, I'm going to make this castle just as it was before."

"BETTER, even!" boomed the Creature. "We could EVEN build a BRAND-new THEATER...."

"GRRRRuKK!" complained Pox as everyone else began to chuckle.

"WAIT! I've got a GREAT idea for a NEW play ALREADY.... I'll call it *STITCH HEAD! A SUPREMELY SPOOKY SPECTRAL SPECTACULAR!* No, WAIT... *IVO! AN INCREDIBLY INVENTIVE INTRIGUE!* No, WAIT...."

The sound rang out from the castle and carried all the way down the hill to Grubbers Nubbin. For the first time in years, the townsfolk heard not the cackling of a mad professor, but the laughter of four friends.

And the snarls of one savage monkey-bat.

VISIT THE AUTHOR'S WEBSITE AT:

www.guybass.com

To Ian
'Cause I wrote this
book in his apartment.
G.B.

To Cath and Leni
P.W.

tiger tales

5 River Road, Suite 128, Wilton, CT 06897
Published in the United States 2023
Originally published in Great Britain 2012
by the Little Tiger Group
Text copyright © 2012 Guy Bass
Illustrations copyright © 2012 Pete Williamson
ISBN-13: 978-1-6643-4068-8
ISBN-10: 1-6643-4068-8
Printed in China
STP/3800/0492/0922
2 4 6 8 10 9 7 5 3 1

www.tigertalesbooks.com